For Mum and Dad

Library of Congress Catalog Card Number 2002000574
ISBN: 0-8118-3492-1

Distributed in Canada by Raincoast Books
9050 Shaughnessy Street, Vancouver, British Columbia V6P 6E5

10 9 8 7 6 5 4 3 2 1

Chronicle Books LLC
85 Second Street, San Francisco, California 94105

www.chroniclekids.com

SUMO MOUSE

WRITTEN AND ILLUSTRATED BY DAVID WISNIEWSKI

chronicle books · san francisco

Is this some lawless lump in leotards? Or a chubby champion of justice?

Suddenly, squealing brakes and squeaking mice signal crime in the alley below.

"Unacceptable," whispers the stranger.

Instantly, he vaults into action.

EEEEEEEEEEEEEEK!!!

ATOYA

CRASH!

The kidnappers' car flattens
into foil.

"SUMO MOUSE!" they howl.
"GET HIM!"

But the villains fight without skill or honor.

BANG!

They fall to his superior technique.

OSHI-DASHI!

TSUMA-DORI!

MAKI-OTOSHI!

"Thank you, Sumo Mouse!" shouts the crowd.

The hefty hero bows, then vanishes into the night.

The owner of Tanaka Toys glares at his defeated henchmen. "We can't make squeaky toys without squeaky mice," snarls Tiger Tanaka. "Why can't you stop this rodent?"

"Because they're using muscle instead of mind!" sneers Doctor Claw. "Has no one noticed that Sumo Mouse appears *only* when the sumo tournament is in town?"

"All this trouble from a wrestler?" Tanaka snorts.

"A *rikishi*," corrects Claw. "One of the best. He might even be Gachinko, the grand champion!"

"Find out," growls Tanaka.

That night, the gangsters hide above the sumo ring.

CRASH!

They see Gachinko slam into his opponent ...

BANG!

then throw him to the ground.

"'Crash Bang?'" cry the crooks. "That's what we heard when Sumo Mouse clobbered us!"

"Of course!" crows Doctor Claw. "Gachinko *means* 'crash bang'—to tackle a problem head on. Gachinko *is* Sumo Mouse! We must give him something bigger to tackle. Something *much* bigger ..."

After the match, Yama the barber repairs Gachinko's topknot.

"You hit like a train," declares Yama.

"Thank you," murmurs Gachinko.

"But a train can be avoided," Yama cautions, "with just a step."

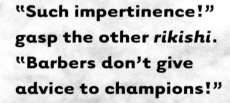

"Such impertinence!" gasp the other *rikishi*. "Barbers don't give advice to champions!"

Yama bows awkwardly.
"Excuse me," he mumbles.
"I have other work to do."

Gachinko shakes his head.
"Yama trained to be a *rikishi* like his forefathers. He mastered every thrust and throw, but never grew in body. Still, he gained in mind and spirit. That's why I listen to him."

"We spoke rashly," say the regretful *rikishi*. "We apologize."

When the arena empties, Yama darts to the basement.

Within a secret room,
a massive suit awaits its owner.

That night, Sumo Mouse frees every captive of Tanaka Toys.

"I'm ruined!" howls Tiger Tanaka.
"Claw! Stop this wretched rodent!"

"Certainly."

Out of the warehouse plods a gigantic
mouse. Doctor Claw sits inside its head,
driving the huge machine.

"Once I defeat Gachinko," he jeers,
"Sumo Mouse will disappear."

"What if he runs into you?" yells Tanaka.

"I hope he does," replies Claw. He opens
the robot's belly to reveal a spinning blade.
"I'm his BIGGEST FAN!"

The next day, the bizarre giant stomps into the tournament.

Tanaka and his cronies watch eagerly from above.

"I'm sorry," the referee says. "You're not on the schedule."

"What a pity!" the giant exclaims. "I've traveled far to fight the great Gachinko!"

"He looks like an honorable opponent," says Gachinko. "Let's begin."

The crowd hushes as the two square off.

Gachinko lunges forward.
Doctor Claw opens the robot.
"HA-HA!" he cries. "Now Sumo
Mouse becomes SUSHI MOUSE!"

Suddenly a masked blur pushes Gachinko aside and
grabs the machine's ankle.

"Uh-oh," says Claw.

The machine crashes to the ground, shaking Tiger Tanaka and his henchmen from their hiding place.

Gachinko helps Sumo Mouse pull the crooks out of the rubble.

Doctor Claw's jaw drops in disbelief. "But, I thought ... No! It's impossible!" he cries.

"Nothing's impossible!" declares Sumo Mouse. He bows to the approaching policemen. "Officers," he says, "take them away!"

Then he disappears as quickly as he came.

Yama helps Gachinko back to the dressing room.

"I should have paid more attention to your advice, Yama," Gachinko sighs. "If not for Sumo Mouse, I'd be Gachinko bits by now."

"I wonder who he really is," says Yama.

"I don't know," replies Gachinko. "But I'd like to show him my gratitude."

"You already have, my friend," murmurs Yama. "You already have."